Saxon Tales

The Witch Who
Faced The Fire

printed using paper that is made from wood grown in sustainable forests. The logging and manufacturing processes conform to the environmental regulations of the country of origin.

Bloomsbury Education
An imprint of Bloomsbury Publishing Plc

50 Bedford Square
London
WC1B 3DP
UK

1385 Broadway
New York
NY 10018
USA

www.bloomsbury.com

BLOOMSBURY and the Diana logo are trademarks of Bloomsbury Publishing Plc

This paperback edition published in 2017
Copyright © Terry Deary, 2017
Illustrations copyright © Tambe, 2017

A catalogue record for this book is available from the British Library.

ISBN
PB: 978 1 4729 2936 5
ePub: 978 1 4729 2937 2
ePDF: 978 1 4729 2938 9

2 4 6 8 10 9 7 5 3 1

Typeset by Amy Cooper Design
Printed and Bound by CPI Group (UK) Ltd, Croydon CR0 4YY

This book is prod ... able forests.
It is natural, ren ... orm to the

To find out more al ... find extracts,
author intervie ... wsletters.

TERRY DEARY

Saxon Tales

The Witch Who Faced The Fire

Illustrated by
Tambe

BLOOMSBURY EDUCATION
AN IMPRINT OF BLOOMSBURY
LONDON OXFORD NEW YORK NEW DELHI SYDNEY

Contents

The Cunning Man   7

The Apprentice   16

The Mistake   24

The Avengers   32

The Cloak   38

The Trick   47

Epilogue   56

1

The Cunning Man

Oh, I know. You like to be warm. Well, let me tell you, I know how you feel. When I was a peasant child in York, then I loved to find a crackling fire, watch the sparks float upwards and see rich gold, amber and rubies in the flames.

Not now. Oh no. Now I'm happy to huddle in a corner and stay warm with an extra shawl. 'Why,' you are asking... yes, I know you are asking that. Why? Why does Ardith Hutton stay away from the fire?

I, Ardith Hutton, will tell you. Children who burn their fingers keep away from the fire. Now I was nearly burned completely. Burned to ashes and burned alive. So you see why I keep away from those terrible tongues of flame.

'How on earth was Ardith Hutton nearly burned alive?' you're asking. Yes, I know you're asking that... and I don't blame you.

Buy me a slice of the innkeeper's best pork pie and I will tell you. And a steaming mug of your mulled wine, landlord, to keep out the cold. Warm wine doesn't scare me the way those hot logs do.

Now, if you are sitting comfortably, I'll

tell you my story. I'll not bore you with my hapless history... well, just a little to paint the background of my picture. There are pictures painted on the church walls. They tell the stories of the saints. I was always staring at the background, wondering what lay over the hills.

Sorry. I am rambling and I said I wouldn't. So. I was born in Hutton, near York. My mother died when I was born. My father moved to York to find work as a tanner – the man who makes tough cow leather into soft stuff for shoes.

There's a lot of filth goes into tanning, you know. In fact a tannery smells so bad the citizens made us live outside the city walls. Dad would scrape off the fat and the flesh from the skins first. If we were lucky there would be some good flesh there to scrape into a pot for soup.

The skins would be dipped into human

pee for a day or two. From my earliest days – as soon as I could walk – it was my job to fetch the waste from the city toilets for Dad.

Sorry. Am I putting you off your roast beef? I'm just saying I smelled very bad. The whole air was bad in our room above the tannery shop. And they say that's what killed Dad.

When a plague came to York, it was the poor who suffered the most. The doctors

said the plague lived in the filthy air of houses like ours. Of course the rich people had homes in the country. They ran off to stay in the fresh air.

The people in the crowded alleys and shambles of York began to die. So first they killed the cats and dogs. 'They spread the plague,' the fools cried.

You can guess what happened then? With no cats in the city the rats began to swarm the streets, growing fat as puppies and twice as bold.

Then the fools started burning herbs in the streets. Vast bonfires of rosemary and thyme, mugwort and mayweed, clover and crab-apple. 'The sweet air will drive out the bad air and we'll all be saved,' they cried.

And you can guess what happened then? You're right. Fires grew out of control and burned down houses. Oh, they were months of madness.

And the maddest people of all thought they should burn down the houses of the tanners like my dad. They wanted our cesspit stink to go up in smoke.

A gang of men and women marched through the city gates and out to our poor wooden house.

Dad would have stopped them but he was too sick. He was sweating till his clothes stuck to his body and his eyes stared out and saw nothing. It was the plague. He ate nothing and drank endless cups of water.

And when the marchers with the tar torches reached us they found me standing by my father's bed, a little girl of five. I was trying to pour water down his throat.

'Burn the house,' a woman cried.

'Burn the house,' the mad mob screamed.

And then a calm voice said, 'Have mercy on the child, you foolish citizens. Can't you see the man is dead?'

And so he was.

That voice of calm came from our neighbour. A stooped and aged man called Wilfrid. And Wilfrid was a wise man of the city. Or a 'cunning man' as some called him.

Ten... twelve... or twenty torches hissed as the rabble raised them ready to set fire to a pile of straw.

'Go home,' wise Wilfrid said. 'Last week we all looked up to the skies and saw flaming arrows fly above the clouds. You all said it was a sign from heaven. A sign that this curse was on the way.'

'We did,' a young wife from Micklegate said.

'Now you are trying to blame a helpless child,' Wilfrid went on.

'Well we can't blame her father if he's dead,' a man grumbled.

'The child will die soon enough, poor, orphan bairn that she is. Burn the house

when she's gone. Have pity, for pity's sake.'
The shamed crowd shuffled off and left
me alone. I was too young to understand
what that all meant. I don't remember now
how kind old Wilfrid buried my poor Dad.
All I remember is I didn't die or burn.
Not then.

And Wilfrid took me in. He was my new

father. And – just like my old dad – I owed
my life to him.

I always knew some day I'd pay him
back. And so it came to pass...

3

The Apprentice

Years passed and I became known as the cunning man's apprentice. To look the part I never cut my hair. When it reached my knees I looked like a wild witch from the woods. It all helped to make people believe I had magical powers.

Every day with old Wilfrid was a wonder of new learning. First he taught me my letters, then I was able to read his old notes and recipes, written on scraps of parchment. I read the labels on the hundred jars he had in his shop.

Jars of herbs and medicines and magic potions.

I had to read every label on every jar and not get one wrong. 'Some are harmless, some are helpful... and some are deadly poison,' he said. 'If you get your mixture wrong, some poor soul will die.'

I learned each drug from linseed, mint, pear, rose and rue, to beet, comfrey, mallow and parsley. By the age of seven I'd learned them all.

When I was around eight years old I asked, 'Why do we have *harmless* herbs, Wilfrid? If they do no harm, and do no good, then why do we keep them?'

He was looking into a ball of crystal, round as a pig's-bladder football that children play with in the street. I knew he called it a 'heahrune' and said he could see into the future when he stared deep into its heart.

He looked up and rubbed his tired eyes. 'Ardith, I am going to tell you the greatest secret of my trade. One day you will take over from me and you need to know.'

'Take over? As a cunning man?' I smiled.

'No. The people will call you a 'haegtessan'... a hag for short.'

'You mean a witch?' I said.

He nodded slowly. 'An ugly word... sometimes they call me Wilfrid the Witch. It makes no difference. So long as we do good they will love us.'

'And if we do evil?'

'They will do evil to us,' he muttered, but he didn't say what shape the people's evil would take. 'Now, you were asking about the harmless herbs?'

I nodded. 'Why do we have them?'

He took a deep breath. 'Sometimes people fall sick and there is no drug we know that will cure them. So we give them

a harmless drug. If they have a pain in the head then we tell them we take swallow chicks and cut them open. We look for little stones in their stomachs, grind those stones up, sew them into a bag and place the bag on the person's head. That's what we tell the sick person.'

'But we don't kill baby swallows,' I gasped.

'Not really. We give the person a powder made of parsley. It doesn't work – neither would a powder of stones from the stomach of a baby swallow – but they *think* it will make their head better, and so it does.'

'We tell lies?' I asked.

He shrugged his bony shoulders. 'Harmless lies. Harmless. But remember some of our cures work. We use a paste made of pellitory to sooth an aching tooth. Now many people don't believe it is that simple. So we tell them to do something silly and they believe it's magic.'

I closed my eyes and remembered what I'd read in the ancient parchment notes. 'We  tell the sick person to boil a holly leaf, lay it on a saucer of water, raise the saucer to their mouth and yawn.'

'Yes, and we rub in the pellitory. The paste works... and they believe the nonsense about holly and the saucer of water works. They go home feeling better... and they pay us.'

And as the months and years passed I learned the true cures and the nonsense.

And what nonsense. For snakebites we rubbed the wound with 'wood taken from a tree grown in heaven'... only Wilfrid and I knew it was from a tree that grew on the muddy banks of the River Ouse. Or to stop bleeding we packed the wound with horse dung. I'll leave you to imagine how helpful that was!

I hated some of the cures. To cure a mad woman Wilfrid ordered her to be beaten with a whip made from the skin of a dolphin. It was so cruel and it didn't seem to work. But some real cures didn't work either – even the true herbs sometimes left the patient sick as ever. For the plague there was no cure.

Of course sometimes we gave the cure and the patient died anyway. Ah, that was when the people turned against the cunning man and his haegtessan.

That is when the priest stood up in church and read from the Bible. He read the words that said, 'You shall not allow a witch to live.'

Again the fools and the fearful marched with torches to burn me in my house. Let me tell you how it came about...

3
The Mistake

Wilfrid was ill. 'What cure can I give you?' I asked as he lay in his bed in the loft.

24

The old man laughed softly. 'Our enemies, the Vikings, have a good story. One of their heroes, Thor, said he could wrestle with anyone and defeat them. An old crone called Elli entered the feasting hall and said she would fight him. Everyone laughed. But in the fight the old woman stood firm and could not be moved. After a great struggle Elli drove mighty Thor to his knees. She said it was a marvel that he had fought so long. For Elli was old age. No one can stand against old age in the end. She always wins. I am facing Elli now.'

I suppose that was the greatest lesson Wilfrid ever taught me. We can cure the sick but in the end we can't cure anyone for all time. 'You can ease my pain, Ardith,' he said, and I found the herbs that helped him sleep.

But still the people of York came

for cures. Wilfrid in his straw in the loft helped me and told me what to do. But one day a woman came to me with a husband who was trembling and feverish. A woman, well fed and rounded with three chins and fingers fat as sausages.

'My husband Oswin here went into the woods last night to catch rabbits. It was a full moon and he never came home. We went searching for him this morning and found him like this – like a scarecrow that has been scared half to death.'

'He has a chill,' I said. 'A fever.'

'That's not what Mistress Grey says. She lives by the woods and she says she's seen this before.' The woman lowered her voice as if she was ashamed. 'Mistress Grey says my Oswin was attacked by elves... and they stole his wits.'

'He has a chill and a fever from the cold,' I told her.

The woman's eyes went narrow and she glared at me. 'You ask Master Wilfrid. He's the cunning man. You ask him.'

'He's sleeping. He needs rest,' I said. Then I made my first mistake. I said, 'But he has taught me all he knows.' Oh, why did I say that? It wasn't true and it was a foolish boast. But the woman's mouth fell open.

'Then when Wilfrid dies you will be the new cunning woman, won't you?' she said, sly as a cat.

'I suppose so,' I said slowly.

'Then you may as well start now. Find a cure for my Oswin, frighted by elves.'

Now Wilfrid had always been annoyed by the peasants' fears of elves and dragons and fairy folk. But sometimes you have to give the people some comfort. Pretend that you believe their nonsense. It makes them feel better.

So I turned to one of the worn leather books – 'The Leechbook' by someone called Bald. Wilfrid used it a lot and said it was harmless enough. I found the page I half-remembered. A cure for someone attacked by elves.

'Here it is,' I said to the woman and pointed to the page. She shrugged. 'I can't read. Women don't get learned how to read.'

I nodded. 'I can gather most of the herbs and potions by tonight. Bring Oswin back then.' Then I remembered he had a chill. 'Keep him warm till then,' I called after her.

She led him away like a sheep on a rope.

I read the page quickly. Too quickly.

Make a salve against elf-kind and night-goers, and the Devil's people.

Take wormwood, bishop-wort, lupin, ash-throat, henbane, hare-wort, haran-sprecel, heath-berry plants, crop-leek, garlic, hedge-rife grains, gith-rife, fennel.

Put these herbs into one cup, and put the cup under the church altar. Sing nine hymns over the cup, boil in butter and in sheep's grease, add holy salt, strain through a cloth. If any elf or night-goers happen to a man, give him this salve, and he will soon be better.

 Fennel. You know it, I'm sure. It's a plant with yellow flowers, isn't it? You grind up the seeds to make a powder that is wonderful for driving fleas away. I'm sure you use it yourself. I read the magic charm and I read 'fennel'... but I saw the word 'funnel'. Yes, I was stupid. I was in a hurry. I gathered a mushroom called 'fool's funnel.'

Fool's funnel is a poison mushroom. Oh dear.

And then the recipe said it was a 'salve', didn't it? You rub a salve into the skin. But I forgot what a salve was.

When Oswin came back at moonrise, I mixed the potion into a drink. Oh dear, oh double dear.

31

4

The Avengers

It was Brecc the Beggar who warned us. Wilfrid had always been kind to the lad. He'd fed him and cured him of the sores and rashes on his body that was thin as a corn stalk. In the whole of York we were the only ones who saw him as a friend. Oh, yes, people threw coins in his cap, but no one stopped to speak to him. Many spat on him, and most wanted him swept from the cobbles on Ouse Bridge like some dead cat.

'They are angry with you and Wilfrid,' Brecc said as he rushed to our door.

Wilfrid was down from the loft and looking better that evening. 'What have we done?' he asked.

'They say you are a pair of haegtessans... witches,' the boy said. 'They say they want to burn your house with you inside. You shall not suffer a witch to live, the priest says. They're coming to get you. Coming to burn you.'

'Again?' I sighed with a faint memory of being a child when Wilfrid rescued me from the people and their burning torches.

Wilfrid rose to his feet and held on to the table to help his weak legs. 'Calm down, Brecc. Tell us *why* they want to harm us when we've done them so much good.'

Brecc swallowed hard. 'Oswin of Monks Bar came to you because he was frighted by elves. You gave him a potion, Miss Ardith. It made him worse. He sat on the toilet all night, emptying his bowels... and when he stopped he started being sick. His wife says you poisoned him because you're a friend of the elves and you want to finish what they started.'

'Thank you, Brecc. We are at least prepared,' Wilfrid said. He turned to me, 'So what potion did you give him and how did you mix it?' he asked.

I told him. He nodded and told me where I had gone wrong. He wasn't angry.

'Are you going to run away?' the beggar asked.

Wilfrid smiled. 'I can hardly walk, lad. No, Ardith can flee. I will stay.'

I snorted. 'Wilfrid, you are a very foolish wise man. Ten years ago you saved me from the fire. I owe you my life. Now I'm going to save you.'

The old man sighed. 'Thank you, Ardith. But I can't stand up to an angry mob.'

'They say there are fifty people with fifty torches coming at first light to burn you to ashes,' Brecc cried. 'Miss Ardith can't fight them.'

I shrugged. 'Oswin's wife said I will be the next wise woman of York. I can't beat them by force, but I can beat them with wisdom.'

I said it calmly. I didn't feel calm. But Brecc gave his crooked smile and said, 'I think you can, Miss Ardith. I think you can.'

Wilfrid looked as pale as a ghost and his smile was even paler. 'How will you do it, Ardith?'

'With magic from one of your books,' I said.

The old man shook his head. 'My potions work on the sick because the herbs work. But there is no real magic. You know that, Ardith.'

'And stones from a swallow-chick's belly don't cure a bad head. But the people *believe* it. And it's the same with magic. It doesn't have to work. We just have to make the people believe we are magic.'

Wilfrid spread his hands. 'So what do we need?'

'Just the hair on my head,' I said. 'Just my hair – and an old Saxon story.'

5
The Cloak

At dawn the next morning the avenging pack arrived. It was led by the priest, a tall man with hollow eyes and a chin sharp as an axe. I met him at the door. 'Welcome,' I said.

'Confess your sins and prepare to die,' he roared at me.

'Would you like to come in for a cup of mead first?' I asked.

'It will be poisoned just as the potion you used to poison Oswin was poisoned.'

I turned to the mob. 'Sorry we can't

invite you all inside but it's a small house. I just want a word with the priest before he murders us.'

'Executes,' he said fiercely. 'It is not murder if I am doing the will of God.'

'That's all right then,' I said. 'Executed or murdered. Will I end up just as dead?'

'Yes... erm... I mean...' he spluttered.

'Come in... and Oswin's wife can come too as she is the one who has suffered. And Brecc who has sharp eyes.' I turned to

Oswin's wife. 'How is dear Oswin?' I asked as I took her plump arm and half-dragged her through the front door.

'A little better,' she said.

'What's your name?' I asked her.

She frowned. 'Garyn,' she said.

'What a pretty name,' I said in a voice as soft as a dove.

'Is it?'

'A pretty name to go with a pretty woman, Garyn. Oswin must be very proud of you.'

'He *should* be proud of me,' she agreed as she pursed her lips. 'But he can say some very harsh things. And when he orders me around I have to stop myself from hitting him with a stool.'

'Poor you,' I moaned.

The priest cut in, 'Stop this chatter. Why do you want us in here?' he snapped.

'Ah, I wanted to explain why it will be

so difficult for you to murder us… sorry,
execute us.'

'We will simply bar the door, lock you
in, and throw our torches on your roof
thatch,' he said.

'Yes,' I nodded, 'but how will you know
we are inside the house when it burns?'

He gave a laugh as harsh as a saw on
hard wood. 'I can *see*, you, witch.' The room
was lit by a single, smoking tallow candle
and it was more dark than light.

I nodded again. 'And can you see Wilfrid?'

'No-o,' he said. 'But that's because he isn't here. He must be upstairs.'

'Or... he could be right here in this room. It may be that you just *don't* see him,' I said.

There is only a table and two chairs in the room,' the priest argued. 'I can see he isn't underneath the table. So he isn't here.'

'He is sitting at the table,' I said.

'I can't see him either,' Garyn grumbled.

I looked at her. 'Garyn, have you ever heard the tale of Siegfried? And how he kidnapped Brunhild?'

Garyn folded her arms across her chest. 'Of course. We all heard that tale from when we were babies.'

'How did he do it?'

'He stole a cloak from the dwarf Alberich. When he wore the cloak he became invisible.'

I gave my warmest smile and said, 'He did, Garyn. And Wilfrid and I have cloaks just like that. Wilfrid is sitting at the table right now, wearing his cloak. Can you see him?'

She peered. 'No,' she said.

'And that proves it works,' I laughed and clapped my hands.

'Oh, it does,' Garyn gasped. 'It *does*.'

The priest nodded. 'I suppose it does.'

'We wear our cloaks often to walk the streets of York and do good deeds,' I explained. 'If you set fire to our house we would be outside and invisible – but alive. We'd have nowhere to sleep. Maybe we'd have to shelter in the church. It would be funny if you burned out house down and we were clumsy and knocked over a church candle and burned down your church... or your house, Sir Priest, when you were inside asleep,' I said.

'Dreadful,' he agreed and his dark, hooded eyes were pools of fear. 'And the people would be left with no cunning man *and* no priest. What would they do without us?' I asked. 'How sad that you plan to burn Wilfrid's house down,' I said.

'Maybe we were hasty,' Garyn said. 'The poisoning of stupid Oswin was an accident, I'm sure.'

'It was,' I said. 'See? Wilfrid is nodding.'

The priest and the good wife squinted at the table and nodded.

'Then we'd better leave you in peace,' the priest said and backed towards the door.

Then Brecc the beggar spoke up. 'It's all a lie. You can't see Wilfrid because he isn't there.'

He was telling the truth, of course. Our friend Brecc had betrayed us... just as I told him to.

6
The Trick

Are you confused? Let me explain. Every true Saxon has heard the tale of Siegfried and the cloak of invisibility. It was easy to fool the priest and Garyn.

But some time later... the next day or the next week... away from the gloom of our room with its spice smells and smoky air, they would start to wonder. They would wonder if they had been tricked. They would come back for proof.

So I told Brecc to betray us. I wanted to give them the proof right then.

'Oh Brecc, how could you doubt us?' I said.

'Because I am not as stupid as I look,' he replied.

'But how can we prove Wilfrid is sitting at the table?' I asked.

'There is a knife and spoon at the table,' he said, 'beside the bowl. If he's really there he could move them.'

I spread my arms, 'Then try him.' I turned to the empty table. 'Are you ready, Wilfrid?' I asked.

There was no reply. I turned to our guests. 'As you know, when he wears that cloak his voice is invisible too.'

They nodded and swallowed the lie like a trout swallows the fisherman's hook.

Brecc cleared his throat. 'Wilfrid... if you are truly sitting at the table then lift your knife.'

We peered through the gloom. There was a moment of nothingness. Then the knife rose in the air. The priest gave a small choking sound. Garyn just gave a tiny squeal and said, 'Now lift up the spoon.'

And the spoon lifted off the table then floated gently back down.

'Why not pick up the bowl, Master Wilfrid?' I asked. It rose, turned around, spilled a little thin soup and settled again.

'I suppose you expect me to clear up after you?' I moaned. A cloth at the edge of the table rose and dabbed at the spilled soup.

Garyn and the priest tumbled out of the door and I heard them telling the people how wonderful we were and that York should treasure us. That we were true magicians... but performed only good magic.

And so the crowd flowed away like the River Ouse under the bridge. I spoke

softly. 'You can come down now, Master Wilfrid,' I said, and the old man climbed stiffly down the ladder from the low loft.

'It worked,' he said.

'Thanks to Brecc,' I said and patted the beggar on the shoulder.

'But how did you do it?' the boy asked. 'I saw the spoon and knife and bowl and cloth move. But you said you have no real magic.'

'I took strands of my hair and lowered them through the rafters. I tied a couple

to each of the things on the table. In the dim tallow-light you couldn't see the hair. Master Wilfrid was in the loft. When he heard the orders he pulled the ends of the hair and made them lift.'

Brecc looked disappointed. 'It isn't magic when you see how it's done,' he said.

'No, and we mustn't ever tell the people how we managed it.'

Brecc's freckled face screwed up tight. 'Oh, I never would, Miss Ardith. I never would.'

And he never did.

*

Winter came and the dank air from the Ouse was too harsh for the old body of Wilfrid. He died soon after Christmas.

The old crone Elli took him – the old age that even the strongest cannot defeat.

The priest made sure he had a fine burial in the church and spoke of the wonderful man we had all lost. Then he said that, while Wilfrid was gone, Wilfrid's wisdom had *not* been lost. He said the folk of York should rejoice – the cunning man was dead, but the cunning woman called Ardith would take his place.

And so I did. He had saved me from the flames when I was a child. I had saved him and his books from the flames and repaid him. Wilfrid left me his books and I studied them well.

But the work of visiting the sick, mixing the potions and growing or gathering the herbs was too much for one young woman to manage alone. I needed a helper who would learn the trade – an apprentice.

It had to be someone I could trust with the greatest secret of all... the fact that some of the old cures worked, if you knew what you were doing, but that some were as real as the steam from a boiling pot. They were trickery, fraud, deceit and as magical as my left foot.

Still, so long as we did no harm, it didn't matter.

Did I find my apprentice? I did. He was poor but honest, had a sharp wit and a good head for learning. Above all he was a good friend.

His name was Brecc. Of course.

We shared the house quite happily. It was snug and warm when the north winds

blew. But you will never get me sitting too close to the fire.

You've bought me a slice of the innkeeper's best pork pie and I have told you my tale. Thank you for the mug of warming mulled wine. Warm wine doesn't scare me the way those hot logs do.

Maybe now you understand why?

Epilogue

Many Saxon towns had their own cunning man or woman. They studied the books of cures and potions – books like 'The Leechbook' by Bald. We can still read it today.

There were magical words the cunning folk said as they used the cures, but they made no difference. It was what was in the bottles and jars and pots and bowls that mattered.

It was a dangerous life for the cunning healers. They were loved when they helped the sick. But when things went wrong a town could turn against them and punish them cruelly.

No one could really make a cloak of invisibility like the dwarf Alberich. It made a good story of the sort that Saxons loved on a long winter's night in front of the fire when ghosts and magic seemed to hide in every corner.

Some of the herb medicines really worked and they still do to this day. Many 'cures' had no real effect but they helped people who believed they would get better. No one could cure the dreadful plagues which struck cities like York in Saxon times.

We are lucky we live today when so many diseases can be cured and we all live twice as long as the Saxon folk.

Still no one can defeat Elli, old age. Maybe one day...

YOU TRY...

1. The play writer William Shakespeare put witches into his play 'Macbeth'. They stirred some disgusting things into a pot to make a spell. The spell let them see into the future. The spell went like this:

Double, double toil and trouble;
Fire burn and caldron bubble.
Fillet of a fenny snake,
In the caldron boil and bake;
Eye of newt and toe of frog,
Wool of bat and tongue of dog,
Adder's fork and blind-worm's sting,
Lizard's leg and howlet's wing,
For a charm of powerful trouble,
Like a hell-broth boil and bubble.

Double, double toil and trouble;
Fire burn and caldron bubble.
Cool it with a baboon's blood,
Then the charm is firm and good.

What magic would you like to do? Make your own spell from disgusting things you might find in a dustbin. For example, if you want your spell to let you win the race in school sports day, then the spell might be ...

'Mouldy custard from school dinners,
Make my weak legs into winners'

2. Imagine you met a wizard in your local park. He says he will grant you three wishes. What would you wish for?

3. Witches in stories are usually old women. This is very unfair to old people and to women. Anyone with magical powers could be a witch. Can you draw or paint a picture of a witch who is not an old woman? It may not even be a human. You can use all the usual signs of a witch... a pot for mixing spells, a pointy hat, a black cat and, of course, a broomstick.

Terry Deary's Saxon Tales

If you liked this book why not look out
for the rest of Terry Deary's Saxon Tales?

Terry Deary's Shakespeare Tales

Meet Shakespeare and his theatre company
in Terry Deary's Shakespeare Tales.